MIKE MULLIGAN
AND HIS
STEAM SHOVEL

STORY AND PICTURES BY VIRGINIA LEE BURTON

HOUGHTON MIFFLIN COMPANY   BOSTON

TO MIKE

Mike Mulligan had a steam shovel,
a beautiful red steam shovel.
Her name was Mary Anne.

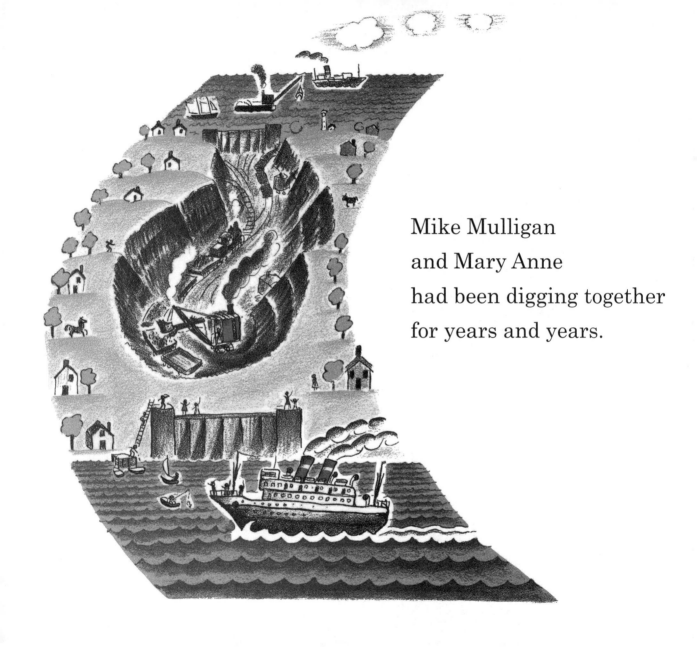

Mike Mulligan
and Mary Anne
had been digging together
for years and years.

It was Mike Mulligan
and Mary Anne and some others
who dug the great canals
for the big boats to sail through.

It was Mike Mulligan and Mary Anne
and some others
who lowered the hills
and straightened the curves

to make the long highways
for the automobiles.

And it was Mike Mulligan
and Mary Anne
and some others
who dug the deep holes
for the cellars
of the tall skyscrapers
in the big cities.
When people used to stop
and watch them,
Mike Mulligan and Mary Anne
used to dig a little faster
and a little better.

Then along came
  the new gasoline shovels
    and the new electric shovels
      and the new Diesel motor shovels
        and took all the jobs away from the steam shovels.

Mike Mulligan

  and Mary Anne

    were

      VERY

        SAD.

All the other steam shovels
were being sold for junk,
but Mike loved Mary Anne.
He couldn't do that to her.

Then one day
   Mike read in a newspaper
      that the town of Popperville
         was going to build
         a new town hall.
            "We are going to dig
               the cellar of that town hall,"
             said Mike to Mary Anne,
            and off they started.

They left the canals
and the highways
and the big cities
where no one wanted them anymore
and went away out in the country.

They crawled along slowly
till they came to the little town
of Popperville.

When they got there Mike Mulligan spoke
to Henry B. Swap, one of the selectmen.
"I heard," he said, "that you are going
to build a new town hall. Mary Anne and I
will dig the cellar for you in just one day."

"What!" said Henry B. Swap.
"It would take a hundred men at least a week."

"Sure," said Mike, "but Mary Anne
can dig as much in a day
as a hundred men can dig in a week."

Though he wasn't quite sure that this was true.

They started in
  early the next morning.
    Soon a little boy came along.
      "Do you think you will finish by sundown?"
      he said to Mike Mulligan.
        "Sure," said Mike, "if you stay and watch us.
        We always work faster and better
          when someone is watching us."

Then Mrs. McGillicuddy, Henry B.
Swap, and the Town Constable came
over to see what was happening, and
they stayed to watch.

Mike Mulligan
and Mary Anne
dug a little faster
and a little better.

This gave the little boy a good idea.

He ran off and told

all his friends in town

and they stopped and stayed to watch.

That made Mike Mulligan and Mary Anne

dig a little faster and a little better.

Clang! Clang! Clang!

The Fire Department arrived.

They had seen the smoke

and thought there was a fire.

Then the little boy said,

"Why don't you stay and watch?"

When they heard the fire engine, the children

in the school across the street couldn't keep

their eyes on their lessons. The teacher called

a long recess and the whole school came out to watch.

Now the girl who answers the telephone
called up the next towns and told them
what was happening in Popperville.
All the people came over to see
if Mike Mulligan and his steam shovel
could dig the cellar in just one day.
The more people came, the faster
Mike Mulligan and Mary Anne dug.

Never had Mike Mulligan and Mary Anne
had so many people to watch them;
never had they dug so fast and so well;
and never had the sun seemed
to go down so fast.
Dirt was flying everywhere,
and the smoke and steam were so thick
that the people could hardly see anything.
But listen!

BING! BANG! CRASH! SLAM!
LOUDER AND LOUDER,
FASTER AND
FASTER.

Then suddenly it was quiet.
Slowly the dirt settled down.
The smoke and steam cleared away,
and there was the cellar, all finished.
The sun was just going down
behind the hill.

"Hurray!" shouted the people.
"Hurray for Mike Mulligan and his steam shovel!
They have dug the cellar in just one day!"

Suddenly the little boy said,
"How are they going to get out?"

Mike Mulligan
looked around
at the four square walls
and four square corners,
and he said,
"We've dug so fast
and we've dug so well
that we've quite forgotten
to leave a way out!"

Nothing like this
had ever happened before
in Popperville.
Everybody started
talking at once,
and everybody had
a different idea,
and everybody
thought that his idea
was the best.

Now the little boy had another good idea.
"Why couldn't we leave Mary Anne in the cellar
and build the new town hall above her?
Let her be the furnace for the new town hall *
and let Mike Mulligan be the janitor."

* Acknowledgments to Dickie Birkenbush.

"Why not?" said all the people.
So they found a ladder
and climbed down into the cellar
to ask Mike Mulligan and Mary Anne.

"Why not?" said Mike Mulligan.

So it was decided,

and everybody was happy.

They built the new town hall
right over Mike Mulligan and Mary Anne.
It was finished before winter.

Now when you go to Popperville,
be sure to go down in the cellar
of the new town hall.

There they'll be,
   Mike Mulligan and Mary Anne . . .
      Mike in his rocking chair
      and Mary Anne beside him,
         warming up the meetings
         in the new town hall.